A NOTE TO PARENTS

Disney's First Readers Level 2 books were created for beginning readers who are gaining confidence in their early reading skills.

Compared to Level 1 books, **Level 2** books have slightly smaller type and contain more words to a page. Although sentence structure is still simple, the stories are slightly longer and more complex.

Just as children need training wheels when learning to ride a bicycle, they need the support of a good model when learning to read. Every time your child sees that you enjoy reading, whether alone or with him or her, you provide the encouragement needed to build reading confidence. Here are some helpful hints to use with the **Disney's First Readers Level 2** books:

★ Play or act out each character's words. Change your voice to indicate which character is speaking. As your child becomes comfortable with the printed text, he or she can take a favorite character's part and read those passages.

★ Have your child try reading the story. If your child asks about a word, do not interrupt the flow of reading to make him or her sound it out. Pronounce the word for your child. If, however, he or she begins to sound it out, be gently encouraging—your child is developing phonetic skills!

★ Read aloud. It's still important at this level to read to your child. With your child watching, move a finger smoothly along the text. Do not stop at each word. Change the tone of your voice to indicate punctuation marks, such as questions and exclamations. Your child will begin to notice how words and punctuation marks make sense and can make reading fun.

★ Let your child ask you questions about the story. This will help to develop your child's critical thinking skills. Use the After-Reading Fun activities provided at the end of each book as a fun exercise to further enhance your child's reading skills.

★ Praise all reading efforts warmly and often!

Remember that early-reading experiences that you share with your child can help him or her to become a confident and successful reader later on!

— Patricia Koppman
Past President
International Reading Association

For my "Beauty," Lauren
Hope, and the beauty
within us all   —G.T.

Pencils by Scott Tilley, Orlando De La Paz, Denise Shimabukoro

First published by Disney Press, New York, New York.
This edition published by Scholastic Inc.,
90 Old Sherman Turnpike, Danbury, Connecticut 06816
by arrangement with Disney Licensed Publishing.

SCHOLASTIC and associated logos are trademarks of Scholastic Inc.

ISBN 0-7172-6457-2

Printed in the U.S.A.

The
Beast's Feast

by Gail Tuchman
Illustrated by Eric Binder and Darren Hont

Disney's First Readers — Level 2
A Story from Disney's *Beauty and the Beast*

SCHOLASTIC INC.

New York   Toronto   London   Auckland   Sydney
Mexico City   New Delhi   Hong Kong   Buenos Aires

The Beast woke up
and out he flew.
"Tonight's my feast.
What should I do?"

The Beast called Lumiere,
who said to the Beast,
"I'll shine brightly at your feast."

"Oh, good!" said the Beast.
"We'll have bright candlelight
at my feast tonight."

The Beast called Cogsworth,
who said to the Beast,
"I'll tick and chime
at your feast."

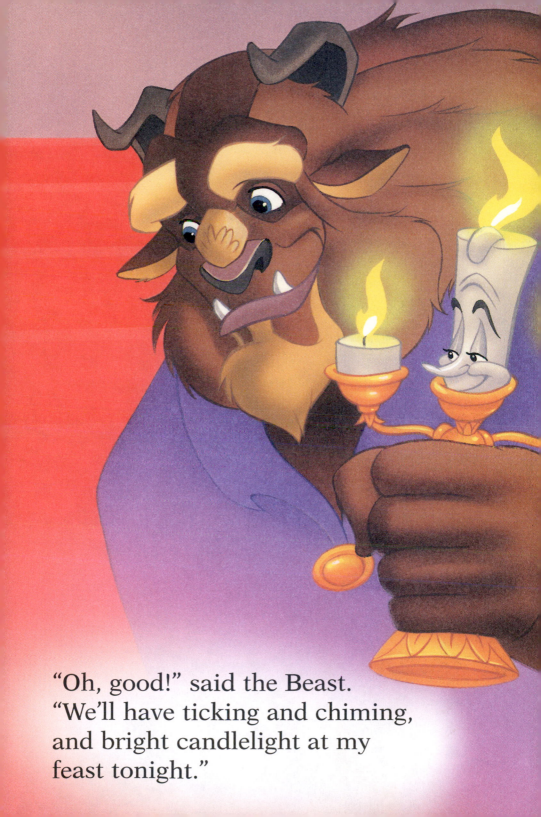

"Oh, good!" said the Beast.
"We'll have ticking and chiming,
and bright candlelight at my
feast tonight."

The Beast called Mrs. Potts,
who said to the Beast,
"I'll make hot tea
for your feast."

"Oh, good!" said the Beast.
"We'll have hot tea, ticking and
chiming, and bright candlelight
at my feast tonight."

The Beast called Chip,
who said to the Beast,
"I'll blow bubbles at
your feast."

"Oh, good!" said the Beast.
"We'll have bubbly hot tea,
ticking and chiming,
and bright candlelight
at my feast tonight."

He called the others.
They said to the Beast,
"We'll come to your feast.
We'll dance and we'll sing.
We'll play and we'll ring."

"Oh, good!" said the Beast.
"We'll have dancing and singing,
playing and ringing, bubbly hot tea,

ticking and chiming,
and bright candlelight
at my feast tonight."

The Beast went up and gave a shout,
"I hope these plans will all work out!"

"Hear that?" said Mrs. Potts.

"Start the fire. Bring out the pots.
Wash the glasses. Wipe off the spots."

"Shine the silver. Roll out the rings. Set the table with all fine things."

Then, out came the rest.
"We'll make it the best!"

"We'll shake. And we'll bake.
Sweet treats we'll all make!"

"Belle," said the Beast,
"Welcome to my feast!"

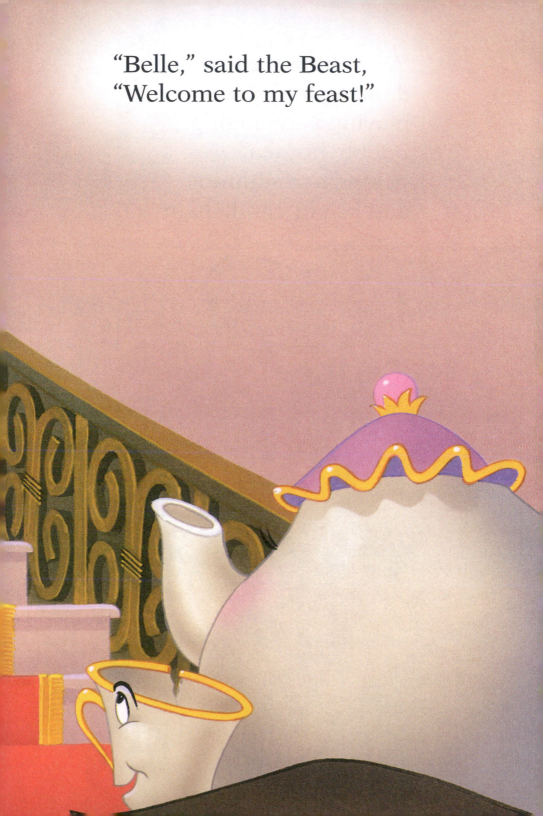

"We'll have treats to eat,
dancing and singing,
playing and ringing,
bubbly hot tea,
ticking and chiming,
and bright candlelight."

The Beast smiled at Belle,
who said to the Beast,
"What a wonderful night.
What a wonderful feast!"

"What a wonderful plan,"
thought the Beast,
"to have a fine feast . . .

for Beauty and the Beast."

Enhance the reading experience with follow-up questions to help your child develop reading comprehension and increase his/her awareness of words.

Approach this with a sense of play. Make a game of having your child answer the questions. You do not need to ask all the questions at one time. Let these questions be fun discussions rather than a test. If your child doesn't have instant recall, encourage him/her to look back into the book to "research" the answers. You'll be modeling what good readers do and, at the same time, forging a sharing bond with your child.

The Beast's Feast

1. **What is a feast?**

2. **What will Chip do for Beast's feast?**

3. **Who did Beast invite to his feast?**

4. **Why does Beast need bright candlelight for his feast?**

5. **What kinds of food do you have at your feasts?**

6. **What words in the story end with the letters -ing?**

Answers: 1. a big, fancy meal. 2. blow bubbles. 3. Belle. 4. because the feast is at night and he needs to see. 5. answers will vary. 6. *possible answers:* ticking, chiming, dancing, singing, playing, ringing.